Patch's Adventures

Patch the Lucky Kitten

Patch's Adventures

Adventures

Patch the Lucky Kitten

by Charlotte Li

FIRST EDITION

ISBNs:
eBook: 978-1-80227-445-5
Paperback: 978-1-80227-444-8

Prepared by PublishingPush.com

For my mum, Anthea and my dad, Simon for all their encouragement and support. Without them this book would have never been born.

contents

1

PATCH THE KITTEN

Patch was a boisterous little kitten. He always climbed when he could, and he was very energetic too. He was growing rapidly by the day. He always tried to explore and push boundaries, until he was found out and was gently chastised by his family.

He lived in a palatial house, which had perfect square windows with bits of ivy crawling prettily over the walls. The front door was Oxford blue, and it had a cat shaped doorbell, which meowed seven times when you rang it. The house had a large, beautiful garden dotted with kaleidoscopic flowers and a nice big apple tree that was shady enough to laze around and sometimes escape from the scorching sun. The lush green grass danced and swirled in the blowing breeze. Green shrubs, adorned with sweet-smelling flowers, bordered the garden with their white roots dug firmly into the soft brown earth. Bees and butterflies stopped to pay a visit to the colourful flowers and occasionally, elegant birds swooped down for the sweet juicy nectar that was hidden deep inside the flowers. Just before the garden started, there was a big stone patio where there was a green garden table and a few chairs.

Patch loved his owners, especially Callie. Callie had two older twin sisters called Mira and Mia and they loved Callie as much as she loved them. She also adored her parents too. Her dad was called Andrew and her mum was called Nancy.

One day, when Patch was exploring, he found a food cabinet with its door ajar. He searched every nook and cranny of the cabinet until he spotted a small, petrified mouse. But unlike other brutal cats that would have pounced straight on it for a meal, Patch carefully picked

up the trembling mouse and placed it
tentatively out into the lush garden. He
bade it goodbye with a small purr and
the mouse squeaked nervously in
reply and scurried off quickly
just in case. Patch thought
he was the luckiest
cat in the universe
to have an amazing
garden. He was about
to set off to laze and
roll leisurely around
the base of the apple
tree as the inviting sun
freckled light across the
stunningly neat garden,

when he heard Callie calling him in for
a meal and a cuddle.

Patch bounded straight through the
cat flap and raced towards his dish.
He was famished. This morning he
had mouth-watering tuna and now
he had scrumptious salmon. Patch
purred contently and he bumped his
head affectionately against Callie's arms
and gave her a kiss on her nose.

2

Patch's Discovery

One sunny day, Patch was strolling along the borders of the stunning garden when suddenly he heard a tiny pitiful meow. He speedily swivelled his ears around and heard it again. He trotted agilely towards the sound and found a small kitten crying and yowling for all it was worth, lying limply on its side. Its white fur was stained in places with mud.

"Don't be afraid, I'm friendly," Patch gently whispered. "My name is Patch. I can take care of you in my home. My family will take care of you too. What's your name?"

The dinky snow-white kitten hiccupped and gently murmured, "I'm Abby. Will you really take care of me?"

"Of course, I will. Don't you worry," Patch chuckled gently. "You're in good hands. By the way, can you walk up to the house?"

Abby looked across from where she was and shook her pretty head. He gently and sympathetically touched her nose with his.

"I will carry you then."

Patch lifted her up in his tender mouth and he walked gingerly to the house. When he arrived back at the enormous house, Patch yowled as loudly as he could, and Callie came running. Patch then lowered Abby carefully onto the cold tiled floor.

With her eyes full of concern, Callie asked, "What's the matter, Patch? Are you all right?" Then she promptly spotted Abby and she exclaimed, "You are so cute, aren't you, baby? I will call you . . . Abby."

She picked Abby up and cradled her lovingly. Abby meowed and bumped her tiny head against Callie's warm arms. Patch's heart jumped for joy; it really

was the perfect name for the cute little kitten.

"I will have to ask Mum and Dad for permission to keep you. But I have a tiny inkling that they will say yes."

Callie ran to get her parents whilst holding Abby to show them how cute she was and persuade them to adopt her. Soon, Callie returned with a big smile stuck to her glowing tanned face as she came rushing in.

"They said yes. They said yes, Patch!"

Patch happily grinned a cat grin and he snuggled up cosily next to Abby and they purred to their caring hearts content.

Soon, Patch's whole family came enthusiastically to fuss over him and

Abby. Abby was a bit hesitant about all the fuss at first but soon felt accustomed to it. They purred like roaring engines as their owners slowly stroked and tickled their fluffy, warm tummies. They flipped around energetically and stretched out even further to be pampered even more.

After all that drama, they went to their cat bed and snuggled together. Before drifting off to sleep, Patch thought once again that he was the luckiest cat in the universe.

3

THEIR DAY

WHEN Patch woke up to find Abby next to him, he felt his loving heart melt at the sight of the tiny kitten curled up snugly next to him. When Abby woke with a tiny sneeze, lethargic from sleep, she looked around at the slightly unfamiliar surroundings and she looked about anxiously, afraid of what had happened. Then she realised where she was.

Safe and sound in
Patch's house.

Callie then greeted
them cheerily with an
early morning cuddle
and fed them both tasty
cod and gave them milk and
water to drink.

After finishing their appetising meal,
they bounded energetically outside
to chase butterflies and let the warm
sun soak through their soft fur. Patch
showed Abby what flowers he loved

the most. They then played tag to wear off some of their energy.

When they got tired, they rested peacefully and dozed under the colossal apple tree where nearby grass twirled and swirled gracefully like a ballerina. The brilliant sun shone as it sent warmth to the whole earth. Underneath the tree, rays of sunshine seeped through the gaps and sent a pretty pattern across the soft grass.

Gradually, the sun got sweltering hot, and the kittens strolled back to the house for the coldness of the tiled floor. Callie saw Patch and Abby and laid out delectable sardines for them. Patch gobbled his up whilst Abby ate at a slower pace.

After the meal, both kittens felt very tired and approached their cat bed. They had a luxurious cat nap and were filled with energy after it. They explored the house together and Patch showed Abby the best places to hide. They spent some time playing hide-and-seek before dinner. In the middle of the game, Callie came searching for them for she wanted a cuddle, and they were glad to let their fluffy fur be stroked by the kind tender hands of Callie.

When dinner was served, the fragrance of cooked prawns filled the air, so Patch and Abby dug in hungrily.

Patch showed Abby how to groom herself clean so that when she was

bigger, she would know how to do
it herself. Abby ended up trying to
chase her tail when she tried to clean
it and Patch tried to control his mirth.
When he finally stopped laughing, he
showed her again how to do it. They
padded around, checking that their
family was safe, occasionally swirling
slowly around one of their owners they
happened to meet.

That night, they jumped onto
Callie's bed, and they snuggled down
with her until she was asleep. Patch
knew they really shouldn't sleep on
Callie's bed but it was Abby's second
night at his house so he thought
bending the rules a bit wouldn't hurt.
The melancholy moon peered through

the half-curtained window to see why it was so jolly in the house.

When Callie's parents popped in to say goodnight to Callie, Patch and Abby were already fast asleep cuddled together at the end of the four-poster bed that Callie owned. Nancy was touched by this scene and allowed Patch and Abby to sleep on Callie's bed if they wanted to. Patch was so happy that he felt his heart would burst with joy.

4

SCHOOL?

THE kittens stretched lethargically from their deep slumber on the four-poster bed. It was only 5 o'clock on a Tuesday, so Patch and Abby decided to take an early morning stroll around the block. After the daily morning wash at the crack of dawn, they slipped out soundlessly through the gently swaying cat flap and Patch helped small Abby up over the fence, and onto the other side.

When they reached the other side, Abby was astonished with the variety of lush green trees, vibrant flowers and multi-coloured plants. She spent lots of time rushing from tree to tree, dashing from flower to flower. The dappled sun sprayed the earthy ground with warmth as it shone high from the aquamarine sky.

When Abby had stopped rushing around giddily, she breathlessly said, "Patch, I've decided my favourite flower here is this pink rose. Isn't it a beauty?"

They both approached the sweet-smelling, pink rose, and inhaled the aroma of the remarkable flower. They noticed the delicacy of the blooming

flower's petals and the prickles of the emerald stem that had strong thick roots burrowing deep into the soft brown earth. They grudgingly tore themselves away from the mesmerising rose and scurried quickly back to the grandiose house and jumped through the swinging cat flap.

Just as they stepped into the house, Callie tumbled down the stairs like a very active whirlwind and they yowled slightly in protest.

Callie looked contrite and apologised, "Sorry, Patch. Sorry, Abby."

They forgave her and started impatiently rubbing and clamouring for food as they were ravenous from their early morning stroll.

Callie laughed kindly and said, "Okay, okay, it's coming. Stop trying to trip me up. Careful!"

She ladled out pilchards – Patch's all-time favourite – into the special bowls for them and it was not long before Abby and Patch were excitedly trying to jump up to the table for the mouth-watering pilchards. She carefully laid the bowls down as so not to spill anything and Patch and Abby earnestly stuck into eating with gusto.

"Mmm . . . delicious!" Patch exclaimed through his big mouthful of pilchards.

Abby replied too with a whole mouthful, "It really is delicious!"

Callie watched with pride as they ate. Callie suddenly looked startled.

"Oh no, I nearly forgot that it was a school day. I better eat breakfast and get dressed," she said. Callie quickly dashed upstairs and into her bedroom to get dressed.

Abby curiously questioned, "What's school?"

Patch answered briskly, "Oh, it's just a place where humans go when they want to get an education which is the process of learning human things."

Abby nodded and seemed satisfied with this explanation. They padded upstairs and found Callie with her sisters. One of her sisters was braiding Callie's long chocolate-coloured hair for school so that it stayed out of her aquamarine eyes. They then proceeded

to rush down the stairs and out the front door but then Callie spotted Patch and Abby, so she decided to fuss over them first.

"I will miss you when I go to school and please be good for me," Callie said. She blew them each a kiss and hurried out the door with her family.

"I'm going to school with them. Are you, Patch?" Abby said.

Patch thought of the consequences of what may happen and decided it didn't matter.

"Sure, I'm going too."

"Let's go!" Abby exclaimed.

They followed Callie and her family all the way to school, all the time a little behind so as not to be seen. Patch and

Abby occasionally slunk off and hid behind bushes or trees when people were approaching them.

They soon arrived at the school, and they were shocked at how many people were there. Callie kissed her family goodbye and prepared to go to her classroom. Patch and Abby followed her, silently slinking and weaving through rushing legs and feet.

When they reached the bright, colourful classroom, they crept through the door just before Callie closed the door behind her. Abby and Patch crouched down under the desk, the one that Callie sat at.

Abby hissed to Patch, "When can we leave?"

"Actually, I'm not sure. Maybe after break?" Patch whispered back.

Abby stayed silent. Patch listened to the drone of the children's voices and was rocked to sleep like it was a lullaby.

5

Afternoon
at School

"Wake up, Patch, wake up. It's about midday now," said Abby.

Patch yawned groggily and snapped awake.

"Oh no! I think we should maybe show up during a lesson," he replied.

Abby nodded.

Soon, the children filed in orderly all

buzzing with the excitement of lunch.
Callie sat down and Patch and Abby
tickled her with their tails. Callie burst
into giggles. She peered discreetly under
the table and had to stifle a gasp.

"What are you doing here, Patch? Abby, why are you here?" Callie whispered barely audible. She sighed but smiled. "I will just have to tell the teacher that you snuck in here."

The teacher confidently strode in, and Callie timidly raised her hand.

"Miss, I found my two cats here right under my table."

The teacher walked quickly over to Callie and peered under the table. Patch and Abby did their best to look cute and innocent and the teacher's heart melted instantly. She reached down and gently stroked Patch and then she stroked Abby's fluffy chest and silently gave a sigh of pure bliss. It was so soft!

Callie's teacher straightened up and snapped back into her usual stern mode and said to Callie, "You can take them to the reception and ring your mum or dad so that they can take them home."

Callie thanked the teacher and hurried off to the reception. She speedily told the receptionist everything and she rang her mum, yet again having to explain what happened. She stayed with Patch and Abby until her mum came to pick them up.

Meanwhile, back in the classroom, the teacher asked if anyone else had a pet and they all nodded yes.

The teacher smiled and said, "Good. That makes it a lot easier then. Now write what kind of pet you have."

She handed out paper to everyone and she soon collected them.

"If you have more than one pet, you will have to choose."

The students murmured and asked what all this meant but the teacher said she would announce it when Callie came back without her kittens.

Callie slipped back into the classroom, barely noticeable to anyone and glided back smoothly into her seat.

The teacher said, "Good. Now that everyone is back, I can tell you my plan. My plan is to have a 'bring your pet to school' day so that your pet can experience a school day. We'll have lots of fun together, providing your pet won't go crazy. I have to say no to crazy dogs."

Luckily, no one had crazy dogs. The children started chattering excitedly but the teacher shushed them.

Callie's teacher said, "I have something else to say too. If you have two different kinds of pets, for example, a dog and a bird, you will have to choose one. However, if for example you have two cats, you can bring them both, provided you can handle them."

Callie was overwhelmed with this news and was flabbergasted. She then came to her senses and her heart jumped for joy. It was a chance for her to let Patch and Abby shine.

The teacher continued, "It is going to be this Friday."

This Friday? Callie thought. *That's*

only three days away. I can't wait to tell Patch and Abby and I am so happy that they can both come to school!

Soon, the loud school bell rang and everyone jumped up, excited. They couldn't wait for Friday to come.

Callie rushed home anticipating the moment when she told her family, Patch and Abby the amazing news. As soon as she opened the front door, she yelled for her mum and dad.

She excitedly squealed out, "Mum, Dad! I can't believe that my teacher actually said that on Friday we can bring our pets to school! Oh, I'm so excited!"

Mum and Dad exchanged a look and smiled. They were excited themselves too but tried to hide their excitement.

After telling her mum and dad the great news, she speedily hunted Patch and Abby down. When both Patch and Abby were comfortably on Callie's lap, she told them the good news.

"Abby, Patch, I can't believe that my teacher said that we could bring our pets to school! That means you two. We are going to have lots of fun!"

Both Patch and Abby meowed and purred as they nuzzled their sweet little heads against their mistress' warm hand and Callie chuckled in the sweetness of all of it.

Callie murmured soothingly, "I knew you would enjoy the news."

When it was an oasis of calm and the whole family had gone to bed, Patch and Abby languidly stepped towards their comfy cat bed and they curled up next to each other. Patch smiled his spectacular cat smile and glanced down at gentle miniature Abby and calmly snuggled up closer to her. Abby purred with cheerfulness.

"How lucky we are to be invited to the school," Patch whispered so as not to wake the family.

Abby nodded and mumbled as she was half asleep, saying, "Yes, we are lucky. I am so glad that you found me back in springtime. Is it nearly summertime?"

Patch agreed, "It's now 24th May. You have come a long way from a little fragile kitten to a fearless bold almost adult cat."

Patch was indeed proud of his adopted kitten, and he was growing rapidly into a full-grown cat. He had speedily learnt to master the act of parenting – he had taught a very obedient Abby to learn all the skills that a cat would need to survive.

Patch's mind wandered and remembered the time he taught Abby to climb a tree so she could escape from the evil clutches of nasty dogs. She had slowly succeeded bit by bit but suddenly she fell with a plop. Consequently, her beautiful round eyes that usually gleamed with happiness, brimmed with unstoppable tears and Patch, kind as always, rushed to her side with sympathy and consoled her.

Abby had glanced at Patch shyly and Patch once again saw in her marble blue eyes that she could express her feelings infinitely in them. Patch's heart

had melted and he kissed Abby gently
on her cute pink nose. Patch coaxed
Abby into trying again and this time
she had flourished, and Patch praised
Abby endlessly. Abby had beamed and
nuzzled her pretty head against Patch's.

Patch sighed contentedly and both
of them drifted silently into sleepy
slumber.

6

Rainy Day

The next morning, the sky was cloudy, and it was raining. Patch and Abby were oblivious of this and waited patiently for Callie to dish up their delicious meal. A slightly bed-haired Callie rushed down the steep steps as usual. Patch and Abby curled their fluffy tails around Callie whilst she was walking, nearly tripping her up in the process. Callie gently chastised them but chuckled to herself as they were irresistibly cute.

When Callie had laid out fresh haddock, Patch and Abby gorged greedily upon the fabulous feast. Callie disappeared upstairs and soon reappeared, only this time looking more immaculate than she did a few minutes ago. She petted them lovingly on the head and was whisked out of the door by her two bigger sisters in fear of being late for school.

Patch and Abby decided to take a quick detour to the garden for a toilet break. When Patch leisurely poked his head out of the transparent cat flap, he immediately felt a series of big fat raindrops dripping on his fluffy head, and he suddenly gave a surprised sneeze. He craned his head up to look and was greeted with dismay. It was raining. Very heavily.

He watched with a heavy heart as the garden began to fill with rain. On the other hand, the grass and the plants hadn't drunk for a long time and were delighted to have the refreshing rain, wriggling and squirming to let the rain soak into the parched brown earth. They joyfully sang their plant song but Patch, disappointed as ever, didn't hear it. The sad sun tried to peek out from the thick clouds, but the clouds didn't let the sun shine through.

Patch retreated into the warm dry house and turned to face Abby to tell her about the disheartening news.

"Abby, do you mind about getting

wet? It's raining outside, so unless you really need it, I recommend that you don't go outside," Patch sadly said.

Abby pondered and finally concluded, "I do really need it, so let's brave it."

Patch smiled at Abby's bravery and nodded his head. They reluctantly stepped out into the wet and dreary atmosphere to do their business. As they did, they got soaked from head to toe in a second; it really was a rainy day. They were forbidden to do it on the spacious lawn, so they had to trail miserably along to the space where the unfathomable garden started. This was one of the times Patch wished the lawn was smaller and the garden nearer.

As they trudged unhappily back
to the house, they met a graceful
little fairy. She had shiny pink wings,
complete with fairy dust, carrying a
miniature gold umbrella and a little
pocket bag. In her other hand was a
golden wand, shimmering despite the
rain. She was shielded by the gold
umbrella and her golden hair framed
her beaming face. Her sky-blue eyes
gleamed and her lips were pink. She
smiled sweetly and angelically at Patch
and Abby and swooped down until she
was level with them. She greeted them
warmly.

"Hi, I'm Sunny the weather fairy
and in Fairyland my job is to control the
weather so that no weather gets out of

hand. I can help you if you want me to. What are your names?"

Patch was amazed but finally found his tongue, "I'm Patch. I'm so delighted to meet you."

Abby was a bit bashful, but she gathered up her courage and said timidly, "I am Abby, nice to meet you."

Sunny beamed yet again and with her joyful voice full of excitement, she said, "Now that I know your names, I can help you." She then stopped and looked a bit embarrassed and said, "Well, that's if you want help, Patch and Abby."

"Of course, we want you to help us, but why?" said Patch.

7

UMBRELLAS

Sunny swirled in the thick air elegantly in delight.

"Do you want to stay dry when you go out in the rain? Do you want to stay dry when others sadly get wet?"

Abby, who had now slowly warmed towards the cheerful fairy, said, "Of course we want to!"

Sunny grinned.

Wow, she is really sunny, always smiling, thought Patch.

"In my little pocket bag, I always carry some magical objects and fairy dust. And in order to help you two stay dry and out of the cold, I have two things to help you. First, you will need a magical umbrella that will protect you and a little bit of an area around you. Secondly, you will need some fairy dust if the magical umbrella's power runs out."

Sunny quickly whipped out the two things from her pocket bag and gave them to Patch. She did the same thing, but this time she gave the items to Abby.

"The fairy dust never runs out, so you don't have to hunt for more if you use it up, but you still have to be careful because you don't know what will

happen if you sprinkle it in or on the wrong place," added Sunny.

Patch looked a bit flummoxed and said, "Sunny, I'm sorry to say but we can't pick the umbrellas up or have anything to carry the fairy dust that you gave us."

Sunny pondered and had a great idea.

"I know," she suddenly burst out, "I can put a spell on the umbrellas to make them float just above your heads and make the umbrellas invisible to your owners! As for the fairy dust, I can attach a little zip pouch to the umbrella and fill it up for you."

She then chanted a string of long words. During that, Patch and Abby nodded slowly, processing the thought in their heads. Abby suddenly noticed the rain wasn't dripping down on them anymore.

"The rain stopped," Abby whispered to Patch.

Patch looked around and said, "No, the rain hasn't stopped but Sunny's umbrella is shielding us! I wonder how we use the umbrella and the fairy dust."

"How do we use the umbrellas and the fairy dust?" Abby asked.

Sunny laughed and it sounded like a bell, sweetly tinkling gently in the blowing breeze.

"Oh, silly me! I forgot you weren't fairies and don't naturally know how to use them. You just say, 'umbrella,

umbrella, over my head' and there you go. If you want to tell it to come off, just say, 'umbrella, umbrella, down on the floor' and it lays in front of you on the floor. Try it!"

Patch and Abby tried and stepped away from Sunny. Their umbrellas followed, and they stayed completely dry! What a miracle!

Patch and Abby exclaimed simultaneously, "That's so cool!"

"I am glad that worked! If you ever have trouble or just want to see me, just call out 'Sunny the weather fairy, send her here', and I will come as soon as I can," she said, beaming.

Patch and Abby exchanged excited looks and grinned from ear to ear.

Suddenly, Sunny's wand tinkled gently and she looked half sad and half happy.

"Patch, Abby, I have to say goodbye to you now. The queen of Fairyland needs my help. I hope to see you two again soon. Farewell."

She blew them both a sweet kiss.

"Goodbye, Sunny. We will miss you." Abby had happy tears brimming in her eyes that were as wide as saucers.

"I wish we could come with you," Patch sighed longingly with a wistful look.

Sunny smiled and said, "You will see me on most rainy days so keep both eyes out for me."

And with that, she swooped and swirled away disappearing in a cloud of fairy dust. Patch and Abby stared after the disappearing fairy dust cloud and wondered if they were dreaming. They then remembered that they were dry and knew this was not a dream.

"How wonderful this is!" Patch exclaimed.

Abby nodded and agreed. They continued their way back to the house, only this time feeling joyful. Both Patch and Abby had a spring in their step, and nothing could stop them from feeling happy.

As they arrived home, they quickly said, "Umbrella, umbrella, down on the floor!"

The umbrellas quivered hesitantly for a moment as if they were making

up their minds then swooped
gracefully down on the cool tiled floor.
They admired their umbrellas with
satisfaction. Patch had an electric blue
one with a silver handle covered in
gleaming lightning bolts that moved
constantly, rotating round and round
the handle. Abby had a pink one with
a gold handle studded with glistening
jewels that lit up if you pressed gently
on it.

Patch and Abby grinned at each
other, still not used to having magic
around them. Patch pushed his umbrella
near the cat bed and Abby followed suit.
They then settled down on the cat bed
having a quick doze before Callie got
back.

When Callie got back from school, she stroked them both and they purred in delight. Realising Patch and Abby may be hungry, she set down two bowls for them filled with salmon flavoured

cat biscuits for a snack and they keenly dug in.

They didn't notice Callie was a bit unhappy, but they did notice there were cuts and bruises over her, but they didn't think about it.

When Callie's family had eaten dinner, they settled down comfortably for a funny movie. Patch and Abby curled up on Callie's lap squishing each other, trying to fit on Callie's lap. Callie just chuckled with a tiny hint of sadness and stroked them both and occasionally helped them up when they suddenly slipped off her lap. Callie's family giggled and laughed at the movie as Patch and Abby dozed dreamily into a deep snooze.

8

CALLIE IS HURT

Patch and Abby woke up to a
normal hectic Thursday school
morning and occasionally gave a
yelp or yowl of protest as Callie's family
rushed around desperately trying to find
something, whilst accidently stepping
on Patch and Abby's tails or paws.
Breakfast was not forgotten for them,
and they weaved carefully through the
fast-moving legs and stamping feet of
the family, unluckily not nimble enough

to avoid being stepped on. But finally they made it through the obstacles and ate what they deserved: pilchards!

Before Callie left, she yelled, "Goodbye, Patch and Abby. Love you and behave yourselves!"

They meowed indignantly. When did they ever get into trouble?

When they had finished eating, they groomed themselves thoroughly until they were as sleek as silk. Patch and Abby curled up together near the fire, as it was a really cold day. They chatted all day long about all the things that had happened since Abby came to the house. They laughed at the funny memories and became solemn at the sad bits and before long Callie and her family came back from work and school.

Callie swiftly crouched down next to Patch and Abby. Patch, being an affectionate cat, saw a hint of sadness in her sea-blue eyes. He repeatedly rubbed his soft head against Callie's leg, and she managed a sad watery smile. With her eyes brimming with unhappy tears, a few disobedient ones rolled down her rosy cheeks and dripped on Patch's forehead. Patch noticed a few cuts and bruises on her and compassionately purred to her in an attempt to cheer Callie up.

When Callie left, Patch said to Abby, "Callie looked really sad. Maybe we should study her this evening."

Abby agreed and said, "I haven't been here for long, but I do know that when Callie is happy, she chatters on and on."

When Callie's mum, Nancy, called everyone to dinner, Patch and Abby trailed behind, closely studying Callie. Usually, when nothing was wrong, she would tell her mum what happened at school while devouring her food and always spoke in a cheerful tone whilst her dad talked to her sisters. But today when they sat down to eat, Callie didn't even offer what was going on at school until her mum asked her.

When Callie had replied, she spoke in a glum dreary voice, and it looked like her appetite was gone. She had only pushed her meal around and it was her favourite! It was fried salmon with carrots and broccoli, but she only took a few small mouthfuls just trying to avoid her mum from asking what was wrong. She only ate some of the vegetables and handed most of the fish sneakily to Patch and Abby.

Normally, Patch and Abby would be delighted to have a few fish scraps but this time, they didn't enjoy them. They felt sad that it was because Callie was upset that they could have her fish. No pets liked to see their owner unhappy, so they tried their best to reassure her.

Patch and Abby twirled their precious tails around her bruised legs, but nothing could really cheer Callie up.

Her mum tried to ask about what was wrong, and she only sorrowfully replied, "Nothing."

When her family helped to clear the plates, Patch turned to Abby and said, "I've got a plan. If we go and visit Callie before she falls asleep, she might tell us what is wrong!"

Abby looked a bit more cheerful and nodded her head saying, "Yes, that should work nicely."

When Callie's family asked if she wanted to play Monopoly, she just shook her head and slouched off to the couch where she curled up and miserably sighed, aimlessly staring far off through the window into the distance and didn't even notice Patch and Abby's meows in an attempt to cheer her up.

The jewelled sky glittered as the melancholy moonlight shone through the glowing square. A few clouds hung in the air and cried compassionately, feeling sad for Callie. Patch and Abby gave up and trailed towards where their family were chatting and taking it in turns to roll the two dice.

Patch handsomely leapt onto Mia and Abby took Mira's lap, springing up delicately. They purred in pure bliss as their other mistresses stroked and gently pulled at their warm fur. They watched with content as their family exclaimed and laughed over the game but felt a twinge of sadness that Callie wouldn't join in. They enjoyed as much as they could, and they gradually felt absorbed in the game and meowed in delight when something was won to someone and nudged them affectionately if they lost a lot of money.

After the game, Nancy suddenly said, "As tomorrow is Bring your Pet to School Day, Patch and Abby will be brought to school by leash because I know that they don't like the cat carrier and I think that they would like to have some time outdoors along the way to school. Is that right?" She turned to them.

Patch and Abby meowed merrily, and Andrew chuckled and reached over to tickle them under their chins.

"It sounds like a yes to me then!"

At 9 o'clock, Callie trudged up to bed, signalling that Patch and Abby should follow her up and put their ingenious plan into action. They trotted up, just a few steps after Callie.

Callie's room was on the top floor with a sloped roof, and it had a pink feature wall next to the bed. Photos and pictures of Patch, Abby, Callie and her family covered most of the walls and glow in the dark stars gave a soft glow, like a comforting hug.

As Callie flopped onto the white and pink bed, she spotted Patch and Abby and motioned for them to come up on her bed. They gracefully jumped up and snuggled up close to her. Callie sighed and stroked them both.

She low-spiritedly said, "These days, when I go to school, the bully in my year called Angelica hurts me and calls me names like 'Coward Callie', and all my friends are too scared to help me so that's why I have cuts and bruises all over me. I sit at the back of the class so that's why the teacher doesn't see my sore bits. I really want to tell the teacher or my mum and dad, but I don't want to be a tell-tale." She paused and sighed again but only this time torrential tears poured down her downcast face and shakily began again, "Angelica doesn't at all look like a bully. She is really pretty, a face like an angel, sparkling blue eyes that just melt everyone's heart, and blonde curls.

When she is bullying people, her heart is as hard as stone. I really don't know why but she just started picking me on the day you two came to school. I hope she stops picking on me. She puts on such an act whenever a teacher looks in our direction and she could almost fool the teacher by saying that I am the one hurting her. She makes sure she is the teacher's pet so that she can get away with murder. She is such a devil in disguise."

Patch climbed up her and benevolently licked her nose whilst Abby was being stroked by Callie. Patch and Abby studied Callie closely and realised that her sores were bleeding and frantically meowed and pointed at

Callie's cuts. She looked bewildered for a second and realised what they were trying to tell her.

Callie groaned, "Ugh, I'll creep out of bed to wash them now. I'll be quick!" She quickly tiptoed out of her room so as not to be noticed.

Patch meowed sympathetically and turned to Abby saying, "I wonder if we will meet that Angelica tomorrow. If we do, we may need a plan."

"Maybe we can find out why Angelica is bullying Callie and if she is bullying other people too," Abby said.

Callie soon returned and kissed them both goodnight. They pondered about this and soon they decided to find out tomorrow. They curled up peacefully next to their mistress and were fast asleep.

9

BRING YOUR PET TO SCHOOL DAY

THe next morning, it was havoc! Grooming things for Patch and Abby were strewn across the bathroom tiles as they desperately tried to escape from having a bath. Callie and her sisters tried to catch them as they dodged their quick-clasping hands.

Finally, a breathless Callie said, "Patch and Abby, I was hoping that because I gave you pilchards for breakfast, you would comply and get into the bath sharpish!"

The kittens then stopped in their tracks for they felt guilty and allowed Callie and Mia to pick them up and gently put them into the bath filled with water. They yowled and squirmed helplessly as Mia and Mira tried to hold them still whilst Callie desperately tried to lather cat shampoo on them.

Finally, when the process was done, they groomed Patch and Abby and then tied a pink satin bow around Abby's neck and a smart bow tie around Patch's. Callie asked Mia for her phone and snapped a few photos from different angles.

She kissed them both and tickled their cheeks and said, "Don't you two look fabulous!"

Patch and Abby exchanged a glance at each other and indeed they did look very smart.

"Okay," said Mira, getting up from her crouched position and stretching, "Callie, you go and get their leashes and harnesses ready while Mia and I go dress ourselves up, and Callie, after you fetch the leashes and harnesses . . ."

Mia carried on, "You should dress up too."

Callie grinned and she put her thumbs up indicating that she got the message. She whisked herself around the bathroom door and went out to the hall to hunt for the leashes and harnesses. Mia and Mira followed suit but only going into their rooms.

When they were finally alone, Abby asked Patch with a questioning look, "Why do we need the leashes and harnesses?"

"Remember yesterday when we left Callie to check on the rest of the family?"

Abby nodded, so Patch continued, "Nancy said that we were going to walk to school, instead of the horrifying cat carrier!"

Abby nudged Patch in delight and he put his head on Abby's.

Callie soon returned with two harnesses attached with leather leashes, and she put Patch's on first then Abby's.

Patch had a navy-blue harness and leash, and Abby had a magenta one. Abby's leash and harness stood out against her snow-white fur, and Patch's leash and harness matched how a gentleman would dress.

"Ready to go?" Callie asked.

They meowed in agreement.

She opened the door and yelled down the corridor, "Mum, Dad, Mia, Mira. Patch and Abby are ready!"

She led Patch and Abby through the bathroom door for they were a bit unsure about the whole new thing. Callie was very kind and encouraging and she coaxed them step by step, praising them frequently. When they reached the bottom of the stairs, their family admired Patch and Abby and snapped shots of them with Callie.

At twenty past eight, they finally strode out of the Oxford blue door and onto the street. It was a totally new experience for Patch and Abby because last time when they were following Callie, they didn't stop to smell the flowers or recognise the road for they were too occupied with getting to school with Callie.

Mira, Mia and Callie were in charge of the leashes and took it in turns to lead Patch and Abby. They occasionally stopped to smell the sweet-fragranced flowers and were sometimes impatiently pulled to move on by Mira, Mia or Callie. They complied reluctantly and soon they arrived at Callie's school. Mira and Mia slipped off to secondary school.

Callie took the leashes in one hand and stood on tiptoe to kiss her mum

and dad. They kissed her back and Patch and Abby were led off to Callie's classroom. They immediately recognised where Callie's class was because it was by far the most colourful class in the whole school.

Whilst walking, Callie said, "We're here, Patch and Abby. Remember to be on your best behaviour."

Patch and Abby puffed out their chests, feeling proud to be VIPs (Very Important Pets). Callie opened the door cautiously so if any pets were free, they would not escape through the door, and she carefully led Patch and Abby in.

10

THE CLASSROOM

THE classroom was just as Patch and Abby remembered it. It was big, colourful and now full of pets. On the whiteboard, there was even a tally chart, as one of the activities for the pupils was to make a chart about what and how many pets they had in this class.

Callie gasped, "Oh, wow . . ."

Indeed, it looked like pet heaven, although some naughty dogs were trying to chase the cats that had irritated them, but the cats didn't even know it, climbing up all the places the dogs couldn't reach. They flicked their tails

annoyingly at the frustrated dogs, who whined and yelped, and ran back to their owners as soon as they heard the cats hissing, tails between their legs.

Callie crouched down and took off the kittens' leashes and let them go, giving them the "okay" sign. They scampered off quickly and made friends with other cats. They noticed that whenever a cat decided Angelica could be friendly and went up to her, the cat was neglected and was left alone in the space where Angelica was, for she inched away slowly, as if the cat had a disease.

She had a cute fluffy Bichon Frise and dressed her up with a blue bow on top of her head. She was most definitely a dog person. They decided that they didn't care and met up with a particularly nice cat called Luna and she belonged to Lily. Lily was one of Callie's friends.

The cats talked about their lives, and suddenly Patch said to Luna, "My owner Callie has arrived home these last few days with cuts and bruises all over, did your owner Lily mention it?"

Luna thought for a moment and replied, "Yes, she did say that one of her friends was hurt and was being bullied, but I had no idea that it was your owner. I'm sorry."

Abby said, "It's all right we just wanted to ask you because, did you see Angelica over there? She is the one that is bullying Callie and since she is so afraid of cats, why not gather up all the cats and surround her until she promises not to bully Callie again."

Luna nodded and they set off to tell

all the cats to do that at break time just before the teacher came in. They had a fun time communicating with the other cats and enjoyed playing with them whilst sharing their personalities, likes and dislikes.

As soon as the teacher came in, she ordered all the pets to be returned to their owners.

"Patch, Abby, come here," Callie called. She made little kissy noises that only Patch and Abby knew and they trotted obediently over to Callie with a look of tranquillity on their content faces. They gently rubbed their heads against Callie's leg and she quickly put the leashes back on them and they compliantly sat next to her leg.

The teacher, who was called Mrs Penelope, called everyone to order and soon got everyone's attention.

"Everyone, silent please," she said, "Now that you have settled down, we will now say one at a time who has what kind of pet. Olivia, you can start."

When the class had finished telling Mrs Penelope what pet they had, she recorded what they had on the tally chart. When the total was counted, it was clear there were a lot more cats than any other pet.

Mrs Penelope announced, "Since we have more cats than any other pet, we will do cat related activities first and learn more about cats. You will see that you have a pile of cat related activities on your desk. During this time, you will be using the information on the board to help you. There are cat breed wordsearches, information sheets and much more."

Callie was so exhilarated to learn about cats and Patch felt like, and knew, he was the luckiest cat in the world.

Whilst writing on the whiteboard, Mrs Penelope said, *"Cats are believed to be the only mammals who don't taste sweetness. Cats are near-sighted, but their peripheral vision and night vision are much better than that of humans so they are excellent at hunting at night. And their long whiskers help them feel if they have enough space to squeeze in.*

Cats mostly have eighteen toes: five toes on each front paw and four toes on each back paw. Cats can amazingly jump up to six times their length."

11

THE PLAN

Just before break time, Mrs Penelope said, "Okay, since we have talked about cats already, we will talk about the second pet that we have the most of." She scanned down the chart and said, "Aha, it is the dog. So, after break, we will be learning about dogs."

When the children filed out neatly with their pets, Callie joined with them, and she let Patch and Abby off the

extending leash. They quickly rounded
up all the cats and reminded them of
the plan. They then quietly surrounded
Angelica who was leading her dog,
Angel, and they moved with her until

Patch, the boldest of them all, tickled her with his tail.

She shrieked loudly and shouted, "What in the world?"

But before she had time to say anymore, Callie rushed over and tried to apologise but was cut off by all the cats' meows.

She understood and said, "Why did you bully me? And just look at you afraid of some harmless cats?" She chuckled a bit, showing off her bold side.

Angelica calmed down a bit and explained, "I'm having a tough time at home, and I just wanted to take it out on someone . . ." She broke down sobbing and between hiccups she continued, "My mum doesn't like me . . . *hiccup* . . . and takes every opportunity to take it out . . . *hiccup* . . . on me. I know it is wrong, but can . . . *hiccup* . . . you please forgive me? I promise . . . *hiccup* . . . I won't bully . . . *hiccup* . . . anyone again. I was jealous . . . *hiccup* . . . of you."

Callie comforted her and fished out a tissue from her pocket and offered it to her.

"I forgive you, but bullying is wrong, and I do need to tell a teacher. Though I hope you will be all right and will not be severely punished," Callie said seriously.

Angelica looked up shamefully and whispered, "You forgive me?"

Callie nodded and gave her a gentle smile.

Angelica pleaded, "Will you be my friend? I'm always lonely at break and lunch so please can you be my friend?"

Callie nodded again and said, "Only on one condition. You will never ever bully people or say anything mean or horrible to anyone again."

Angelica beamed and threw her arms around a very surprised Callie. They then led Patch, Abby and Angel around telling everyone that they were friends and how Angelica had stopped bullying people.

At first, Angelica was hesitant, and she stuttered as she was still hiccupping from crying. Angel was a sweet dog, though she had a habit of chasing cats, but Patch and Abby dodged out of the way just in time and Angel was outnumbered.

When the loud school bell rang but softer than normal to try its best to not frighten the animals, it failed. Most pets jumped in shock and their owners desperately tried their best to comfort them. Only Patch and Abby remained unfazed and nuzzled Callie's leg for reassurance. Patch and Abby were led by Callie to their classroom and lined up neatly next to it, waiting for the teacher to arrive.

Mrs Penelope popped her head out from the classroom door and motioned for them to come in. They soon sat down in their usual seats.

"On your desks, you will find some dog-related activities and like this morning you will find information on there."

Angelica was very focused on this session for she had a dog and listened keenly to what Mrs Penelope was saying whilst writing on the board.

"Their sense of smell is at least forty times better than ours. Some have such good noses they can sniff out medical problems. Dogs can sniff at the same time as breathing. Some dogs are incredible swimmers. Some are fast and could even beat a cheetah! Dogs don't sweat like we do."

The lunch time bell gonged loudly, and Mrs Penelope announced, "After lunch, we will be learning about birds and fish: the last two pets in our chart."

There was a flurry of scraping chairs and continuous chatter hung in the air. Patch and Abby were led to the canteen and my, it was loud! A cacophony of noise hung in the air as delicious smelling lunches were opened one by one.

Callie sat down at one end of the table and Angelica sat next to her. Callie opened a tin foil package and inside were two scrumptious salmon! She put them in two bowls and Patch and Abby dug in hungrily. Angel had some dog biscuits though she kept whining for more until she got it.

PATCH THE LUCKY KITTEN

Callie and Angelica talked about everything, gradually warming to each other. Callie's mum packed her: a strawberry jam sandwich, a cupcake (which she shared with Angelica), salt and vinegar crisps, and a juice box; grape flavoured. Angelica's lunch was slightly different: a ham and cheese sandwich, a few jammy dodgers (she gave one to Callie to share), prawn cocktail crisps, and a juice box; apple flavoured.

They laughed and chatted then headed to the gravel playground. They let Patch, Abby and Angel off their extending leashes and let them explore. They sniffed out the fashionable flowers and rolled around a big oak tree. Callie

and her friends played tag and their
pets could help "catch" the others.
They laughed and joked and ran around
trying not to get caught and soon they
were panting hard but they had a lot of
fun.

A teacher then suddenly blew a
whistle and all the children sighed
but obediently lined up next to their
classroom doors and soon filed in.
Callie quickly told a teacher about
the bullying and Angelica was strictly
but understandingly scolded and her
mum was phoned, despite Angelica's
protests. Angelica's mum was ashamed,
promising that she would try to be
kinder to her.

12

Home Sweet Home

When they were all seated, Mrs Penelope smiled and said, "Okay, on your desks are fish and bird activities. We will complete these this afternoon. I will be writing facts about fish and birds so any information you need will be right on the whiteboard."

Slowly, Mrs Penelope's neat handwriting appeared on the whiteboard.

Fish Facts:

There are over 30,000 species of fish in the world and there still may be other species not yet discovered. Fish breathe through their gills to get oxygen. Most fish don't have eyelids, so they don't close their eyes when they sleep. Fish are cold-blooded. Scales help fish to swim agilely and speedily. Fish are vertebrate animals so that means they have a spine. Fish can talk to each other.

Bird facts:

There are 10,000 species of bird some even weighing only 2.6 grams. This bird is called the bee hummingbird. All birds lay eggs to have offspring. Some birds migrate to other countries but some don't. All birds have feathers, and that makes birds special. Birds don't have teeth. Birds are amazing communicators. A group of birds is called a flock, feeding and flying together. Some birds, like a parrot, can mimic humans.

The children used the information on the board and worked almost silently,

with an occasional gossip or to check
answers. They then carried on with
a game of "pass the animal". Mrs
Penelope had brought a toy lizard along
and they had to pass it around. Whoever
had it when the music stopped had to
tell a fact about any animal they could
think of. They had a good laugh but
soon, it was time to go home.

Mrs Penelope shouted over the noise
as she dismissed the class, "Have a good
weekend, children!"

Children ran out excitedly and
rushed off in different directions and
a cacophony of noise hung in the air
whilst they whooped and cheered for it
was finally the weekend. Callie, Patch
and Abby sauntered proudly towards

their family and as Mia and Mira held Patch and Abby's leashes, Callie embraced her parents and squealed, eagerly jumping around.

On the way back home, Callie told her parents everything that happened today including where she and Angelica had made up and became friends. She nattered on and on and her parents listened intently to her; their expressions changing at each event. Mia and Mira kept a firm hold on the leashes in case either one of the cats took it in mind to race off up a tree.

As they arrived back home, Nancy took her front door keys from her jeans pocket. On the keys hung an elegant white cat head keyring. Mia and Mira had matching ones, but Callie wasn't old enough to have keys to the house yet. She would soon get them on her eleventh birthday. They entered through the door and Callie crouched down to unclip the harnesses and leashes.

She smiled and whispered to them, "You can go now."

They took off immediately and speedily ran to the food bowls, and meowed impatiently for they were starving and, of course, there was no food in their bowls. Callie and Mia put cold cooked salmon in the bowls whilst Mira put away the harnesses and leashes. Nancy and Andrew tidied up from what was left of the food as the three girls and the cats scurried away to play.

Callie showed Mia and Mira her cuts and bruises, and they gasped in sympathy. Mia fetched some cream and Mira grabbed the plasters. They carefully spread the cream on the cuts and for the really sore ones, they tentatively put plasters on them.

Callie hugged her sisters thankfully and said, "Thanks, sisses. Should we go find toys for Patch and Abby now?"

They searched high and low for the toys and Patch and Abby joined in. At last, when all the toys had been found, they settled down cheerfully, giggling at Patch or Abby's antics, teasing them slightly as Mia whisked away the toy bird just in time and luckily Abby landed perfectly on her dainty feet. Patch had taught her well on how to survive. Patch now looked fondly at her, and Abby smiled at him sweetly.

Patch thought, *I really must be the luckiest cat in the whole wide world.*

When dinner rolled round, Nancy called, "Dinner time!"

Mia rushed out of the room, but then poked her head back through the doorway, she asked excitedly, "Are you coming? It's penne carbonara tonight!"

Callie yelled, "Yes, I love penne carbonara!"

In response, Callie's stomach growled in hunger. Callie and Mia rushed down the carpeted stairs with Patch, Abby and Mira following close behind. Callie jumped down the last two steps and made a large thumping noise. She rushed quickly to her seat and plopped down, staring greedily at her plate, piled high with creamy penne carbonara.

Andrew had laid out tuna for Patch and Abby today and they feasted on

it, relishing its delicious taste. Nancy said grace and the children shovelled mouthfuls of carbonara into their mouths.

"Woah, slow down and eat it, not shovel it down like a pig," their dad said.

The children smiled apologetically and slowed down. When they finished eating, they spent time looking at the albums from when Mia and Mira were born to when Callie was born and to now. They oohed and aahed at several pictures, laughing at all the funny memories and becoming sombre at the sad memories.

Soon, at half past nine, Callie was sent up to bed with Patch and Abby and her mum accompanied her. Callie climbed under the silky covers of the blanket and her mum lovingly tucked her in. Nancy's soft fingertips stroked

Callie's rosy cheeks and she leant down to give her daughter a kiss.

Callie hugged her mum and said, "I love you, Mum."

Nancy smiled and said, "I love you too."

Patch and Abby jumped on either side of the four-poster bed and Callie's fingers entwined into their soft fur, creating a loving atmosphere that hung in the air. Her mum walked out of the room, and she turned out the light whilst the glow from the stars glimmered softly.

Patch purred contently as Callie's strokes became more frequent as Patch and Abby curled up leisurely beside Callie. As they were about to drift off to sleep, Patch's mind wandered. He wondered what adventures may come in the following days, weeks or even months. He nuzzled Callie softly and drifted off into a deep slumber.

CHARLOTTE LI'S BIOGRAPHY

Hi, I'm Charlotte Li and I am 10 and a half years old. I love to read, write stories and spend time with animals, especially cats and kittens. That is why my first ever book is about cats. I just love writing and when an idea comes to me, I write it down and let it flow. I hope you enjoy reading my books!